DISNEP
VILLAINS

THE QUEEN

Written by
Steve Behling
Illustrated by the
Disney Storybook Art Team

"Magic Mirror on the wall,
who is the fairest one of all?"
It does not have to say anything.
I already *know* the answer.

I am the fairest one of all.

Me, the Queen!

I live in a castle.

I make my wicked plans.

I like to think evil thoughts
all day long.
Who knows what terrible
things I might do?

What is that awful noise?
I run to my window. I see
children playing outside.
Oh no!

I walk outside
and yell, "Begone!"
The children run away.
Oh, I hate being outside.
The sun is far too bright!

I want the rain to last.

It is not raining now.

It makes me mad.

Maybe I can cast a magic spell.

The spell will make it storm again!

I need spiders for my spell.

I walk to the wishing well.

I see spiderwebs.

There must be spiders here!

But when I look inside,
all I see are cute ladybugs!
"Go away, ladybugs!" I shout.

I will use rats for my spell.
I look for the rats.
But all I find are cute
chipmunks!

You can never find a rat
when you need one.
I think a lizard will work.
But all I see is a cute bunny!

I think about the last time
I made a storm.
I was so happy in the rain.
Thinking about how happy
I was makes me very angry.

I go inside the castle.
"Magic Mirror on the wall,
you are no help at all!"
Why do I have a Magic Mirror?
It cannot even make it rain.

I look in my spell book.
There must be something here
to make me feel happy.

Then I find it: the *perfect* spell!
"This will be even better
than a storm!" I shout.

I mix the magic potion.
I drink all of it.

I start to change.

I am no longer a beautiful queen.

I am now a scary witch!

I mix another potion.
I dip an apple into it.
I pull the apple out.
It looks like a skull.
It is a magic apple now!

I go for a walk with
my magic apple.
I see some vultures.
Buzz off, vultures!
This apple is not
for you!

The apple is very special.
Anyone who takes a bite
will fall asleep forever.
I cannot wait to give it to someone!

I cannot give the apple away.
Horrible dwarfs find me.
They are riding cute animals!
Ugh!
They make me drop the apple.

I run to the top
of a mountain.
It starts to rain. I did not even
cast my rain spell!
I am so happy!

I leave the Dwarfs.
I go back to my castle.
"Magic Mirror on
the wall, who is the
happiest one of all?"

Why, it is me, of course!
What spells will I cast
tomorrow?

DISNEY VILLAINS
MALEFICENT

Written by
Steve Behling
Illustrated by the
Disney Storybook Art Team

Welcome, my friend!
I see you have entered the forest.
It is only a short walk
to where I live.

See this castle?
It belongs to me.
You must cross a rickety
bridge to get there.

When you arrive,

a stone raven will come to life.

The Raven will say, "Caw! Caw!"

He will tell me that I have a guest.

Who am I?

Why, I am Maleficent, of course.

I am a very powerful fairy.

How powerful am I, you ask?

Sit back, and I will tell you.

I can do all kinds of magic.
For example, I talk to birds.
They obey my every word.

I also have many helpers.
They are creatures who
do anything I ask.
If I tell them to scare someone,
they will!

Today my pet raven tells me
about a party at the king's castle.
"Why was I not invited?" I wonder.
Perhaps I shall go for a visit!

My magic lets me travel
anywhere.
In a flash of green fire,
I appear inside the king's castle.
Everyone is scared of me.
That is just the way I like it!

"Why did you not invite me?" I ask.
The king orders me to leave.
Who does he think he is?
I will show this king who is
really in charge.

Then the king orders his guards
to capture me.
Simple guards catching
the most powerful fairy?
I laugh and cast an evil spell.

In a flash of green fire,
everyone turns to stone.
The people at the party
have become statues!

"If anyone does not wish me
to be here, speak up." I laugh.
No one says anything, of course.
Statues cannot talk!
You know, I can be funny.

I soon grow bored of my trick.

I reverse the spell.

Everyone is back to normal.

But if you thought they
were afraid of me before,
look at them now!

What a fun party!

I am so glad that I went.

But now it is time for me

to go home.

I have something important to do.

You see, before I left the party,

I played *another* trick.

I brought someone to my castle.

Who is it, you ask?

The prince escapes from my prison!
But I can change into a fearsome
fire-breathing dragon.
Just let the prince try to get past *me*!

I chase the prince to the edge of
a cliff.

He has a shield and a sword.

I am a mighty dragon.

He does not stand a chance!

61

I allow the prince to leave.
He will tell his father
to invite me to every party.
Now I wish to tell you a secret.

I do not want to go to every party.
I do not want to go to *any* parties!
I just do not like it when
people do not invite me to parties.

It is time for you to leave.
Goodbye . . . until next time!

VILLAINS
QUEEN OF HEARTS

Written by
Steve Behling
Illustrated by the
Disney Storybook Art Team

Greetings, loyal subjects!
I am the Queen of Hearts.
I rule all of Wonderland.
Welcome to MY story about ME!

Being QUEEN is hard work.
That is why I sleep all night.
A queen needs her beauty rest!

When I wake up, I must get ready
to greet my subjects.
Now where did I put that crown?

While I am getting ready,
my card soldiers train.
I make them run through
a maze every morning.
Why? Because I can. That is why!

Do you like PARADES? So do I!
That is why I have a parade
each and EVERY morning.

RED is my favorite color.

I love red so much.

I want to see it EVERYWHERE!

If something is not red, my cards
PAINT it red!
My cards are good painters . . .
or else it is off with their heads!

After a busy morning,
I like to have a SNACK.
Sometimes the White Rabbit
brings me berries to eat.

Sometimes the berries are
so YUMMY in my tummy
I could eat them all day long!

But other times, the berries are
NOT so yummy.
Then I become angry!
When this happens,
the White Rabbit runs away.

The White Rabbit comes back.

He brings me a cupcake.

First I am happy.

But when I try to take a bite . . .

it is NOT a cupcake after all!

Now it is off with his head.

"Off with his head!" I yell.

Lucky for the White Rabbit,

I do not stay mad for long.

After all, I am a kind queen.

After my snack,
I like to get some exercise.
A good game of croquet is just
the thing . . . if only those cards
would stay still!

I like to play
against the White Rabbit.
He tries to win the game.
But he will NEVER beat me.
Because I am the QUEEN!

Ask almost anyone,
and they will tell you.
I am the BEST croquet player
in Wonderland!

But the Cheshire Cat does not agree.
HE thinks he can make me lose
with his tricks.
But he is WRONG!

Oh, that cat makes me so MAD!

Why, I could just scream.

You know, I think I WILL!

"Off with his head!"

That is what I like to say.

"Off with his head!"

I could say that ALL day!

Oh, no! Would you look at the time?
It is late afternoon already!
That means it is TRIAL TIME!
I like to hold three trials every day.
It keeps everyone on their toes!

Trials are so much FUN!

I get to say,

"Off with their heads!"

I wish I got to say that

more often.

Oh, well.

We cannot have

everything we want.

Well, except for me.

I AM the queen, after all!

It has been a VERY long day.
There were so many games,
treats, and trials.
I must get some sleep!
But what is that?

I hear STRANGE sounds.

They keep me awake.

I get out of bed.

What could they be?

Oh, how silly of me!
It is only the creaking of my
heart-shaped rocking chair.

I do so love hearts, you know.
They make me so HAPPY!

In fact, they make me SO happy
I scream, "Off with their heads!"
It is a perfect end to a perfect day.
At last I am ready to sleep.
Oh, it is GOOD to be the queen!